PODGE AND DODGE
THE RESCUE

Second Edition

By
Joseph Patrick Cronshaw

Podge and Dodge Children's Book Publishing
PO Box 251
Newton-le-Willows, Merseyside
United Kingdom, WA12 2BE
http://www.podgeanddodge.co.uk

First Edition
Published in the USA
by
Eloquent Books
An Imprint of AEG Publishing Group
645 Third Avenue, 6th Floor - 6016
New York, NY 10022

Published by Podge and Dodge Children's Book Publishing
PO Box 251
Newton-le-Willows, Warrington
United Kingdom, WA12 2BE

Publisher's website: http://www.podgeanddodge.co.uk

ISBN: 978-0-9567768-1-5

Printed in China

Illustrations Art, Cover Art,
Podge and Dodge Characters and Book Layout
Designed by Kalpart Team

In Loving Memory
of
Teddy and Molly
(Dad)   (Mum)

Once upon a time, there lived two clever little elves named **PODGE AND DODGE**. They were well known for their kindness and good deeds, so it was no surprise when a messenger of the King called one evening and told them His Majesty wished to see them, without delay.

As they came out of their toadstool homes, **PODGE** looked at his friend's badly patched suit.

"Surely, you must have a better suit than that you could wear to meet your King. Have you no pride?"

DODGE was a little hurt and replied, "I can't afford a new suit, and anyway I am sure the King has not sent for us to inspect my clothes." Podge realized he had offended his best friend, and he quickly apologized for his bad manners.

"Oh, that's alright," Dodge said. "I don't want to argue with you. Perhaps I will have a better season this year with my herb picking. Then I will buy a new suit."

Arriving at the **PALACE**, they were escorted to the main room, where **THE KING** was surrounded by his Ministers. They all looked very worried indeed. With a wave of his hand, the King cleared everyone from the room, except his War Minister and, of course, Podge and Dodge. Speaking to his visitors in a soft voice, he said, "I have sent for you to ask for your help."

He hesitated for a moment before going on. "You see, my youngest daughter, the **PRINCESS ZARA**, was kidnapped last night by the Goblins. And, although I have sent my bravest soldiers, they have been caught and thrown into the dungeon. So, you understand, there is a great deal of danger. I am putting my trust in you, my friends, to think of a way to succeed in rescuing my daughter."

Dodge had glanced at the War Minister during the speech and did not like the sly little smile he tried to hide. Dodge looked at the King and told him  they were willing to try to rescue the princess. "But surely you are going to explain to his Majesty, the plan that you hope will accomplish **THE RESCUE**," remarked the War Minister.

Dodge ignored the WAR MINISTER and turning to the King, explained that they would like their plan to remain a secret, and that they hoped the King would still trust them to do everything possible to rescue Princess Zara and the other prisoners.

"Of course, you have my trust, but please make haste to get to Goblinland by dusk tomorrow, or it could be too late," pleaded the King.

As the elves left the palace, Podge said, "You certainly did not hide your dislike for the War Minister. Not that I blame you. I was not keen on him either."

Dodge admitted that he had a strong suspicion that they should think of a way to reach Goblinland much earlier than expected.

With a mischievous chuckle, Podge made a wonderful suggestion: "At this time, GOGGLE THE OWL should be in his favorite tree not far from here. If I do my owl call, he should hear me and he could fly us to Goblinland."

"That's good thinking!" Dodge said, doing a little dance of delight. "Well, hurry up, and do your owl call then."

PODGE placed his tiny hands over his mouth, and did a very good owl call indeed. Within minutes came a flutter of wings, and Goggle landed beside them.

After hearing their story, Goggle was more than pleased to help. He told them he would get them to Goblinland within the hour. Overjoyed, the elves climbed onto Goggle's back and very soon were speeding through the air to carry out their important and dangerous mission.

As they were traveling, Goggle felt he had to ask them a question that puzzled him about the Goblins. "Why should the Goblins do such a thing, when they are elves just like you?"

DODGE explained, "Oh yes, they were elves at one time, but they became rebels and caused a lot of trouble in Elfland until the King had no alternative but to send them into exile."

Goggle gave a hoot of satisfaction and seemed to put on extra speed, to the delight of his passengers.

"I can see the lights down below," Podge shouted. "We must be there!"

Goggle told them to remain calm, because he wanted to circle the castle to find the best landing spot for them to gain entry. He noticed an open window and glided gently onto the windowsill. Goggle made sure no one was in the room, then gave the elves the nod to enter. Whispering, he wished them luck and told them he would be nearby in a tree waiting for their call to carry them away from danger.

Podge lit his tiny torch to get a better view of the room, and the elves were shocked at the dust and old clothing scattered on the floor and then the light shone on a door. Dodge crept over and slowly opening the door, peered out and saw the door led to a passageway. At one end he saw a group of Goblins who looked as if they had never had a bath and their clothing was in very ragged condition.

He tiptoed back into the room and closed the door silently behind him. Turning to Podge with a broad grin, he said, "I've got the answer. We will dirty our faces and hands, and put some of these old clothes on over our own. We can then pretend we are Goblins, and we will be free to search the castle for the dungeons." And so they dirtied their faces and hands and put on some of the old clothes.

Soon they were mingling with the goblins. Everyone seemed to be moving in the same direction, making for the big hall. Podge and Dodge followed cautiously at the back, listening to the conversations. As the elves were about to enter the hall, Dodge recognized the Leader sitting in a chair of honor. Worried that the leader might recognize them, Dodge grabbed Podge and hid with him in a small recess in the passage. Podge did not ask why, as he guessed his friend had a good reason and they could still hear every word from the big hall.

The Leader began to speak: "My faithful followers, I am pleased to see so many of you at this meeting, which will, of course, be ended with a tasty meal of herb soup. But first let me give you some exciting news I've just received by carrier pigeon." Here he broke into a peal of laughter, which lasted for several moments. Then, wiping tears from his eyes, he went on.

"The news is from my friend who is THE WAR MINISTER IN ELFLAND. It says that Podge and Dodge should be arriving here tomorrow evening to attempt to rescue the princess and the other prisoners."   With this, he burst into laughter again, as did his followers.

Dodge, with a determined look, turned to Podge and said, "Come on, let's hurry and find the kitchen. I intend to succeed in this mission, whatever the cost." Quietly, they ran down several passages, until Podge pointed to a door and whispered excitedly, "It's here! I can smell the cooking."

They tiptoed to the door and quietly opened it. Peering inside, they found it empty, except for a long table on which there were soup bowls and a large pot filled with soup hanging over a fire on the stone floor.

"Oh, what a stroke of luck!" said Dodge. "There is nobody here." He moved toward the hanging pot, got out one of the little bags he carried around his waist, and emptied the contents into the soup, followed by a swift stir.

Suddenly the elves heard voices and footsteps in the passage. Podge looked around for a place to hide, and, seeing a large, old basket in the corner, he seized his friend by the arm and they both ran and scrambled inside. Just in time, the door opened, filling the kitchen with chattering **GOBLINS**.

"Now there is no need to push. You will all get your share," bellowed the Leader. The two elves watched through the basket weave as the soup was passed around. The Leader gave an order for some to be taken down to the sentry guarding the prisoners.

"Everything is going to plan," whispered Dodge. "Dare I ask what it was you put in the soup?" asked Podge with a grin. Dodge looked at him in surprise, and with a little chuckle, he answered, "I thought you would have guessed. It was my sleeping powder." In reply, Podge gave a little giggle.

As the elves watched through the basket, the minutes passed until soon the Goblins began yawning and then finally slumped into a deep sleep, snoring loudly. The elves jumped out of their hiding place and, carefully stepping over the sleeping Goblins, ran from the kitchen, searching along the passages for steps that would lead down to the dungeon.

Suddenly Podge found the steps through an archway and gave a low whistle. Dodge came panting to his friend's side, and together they made their way down to the dungeon. There they found the guard sprawled on the floor in deep slumber. Podge took the keys from his belt and opened the cell door releasing the prisoners, who were overcome with joy to see these TWO BRAVE FRIENDS.

"Come quickly, Your **HIGHNESS**," said Dodge. Taking the princess gently by the arm, he led her hurriedly through the passages with Podge and the happy soldiers following closely behind. At last they reached the room from where the elves had entered the castle. They took off their ragged disguises, much to the amusement of the princess at their cleverness.

She must have noticed how patched Dodge's suit was, but, of course, she made no comment.

Podge climbed up to the window and, opening it wide, gave a loud hoot signal for Goggle to come and carry them to safety. Soon they heard the flutter of wings — much louder this time, the reason being that Goggle had brought three friends. "Hoot, hoot," he said. "I had a feeling you would succeed, so hop aboard all of you and my friends and I will have you all home before dawn."

What a greeting they received when they entered the palace! The King could not help crying with joy. To show his esteemed gratitude to the TWO BRAVE ELVES, he announced that a ball would be held in their honour, in three days time.

After all the fuss had died down, Dodge took the first chance that came to speak to the King about the treacherous War Minister. The King, red in the face with rage, ordered the guards to seize the wretch and lock him up in the dungeon. He would deal with him later.

Now it was almost dawn, which meant that all elves should be in bed. Podge and Dodge received some wonderful gifts from the King before they departed. But the greatest gift of all came for Dodge two days later. It was a lovely new suit made by the princess herself. What a handsome elf Dodge was when he attended the ball!

THE END

This illustrated children's story is the second in the series of six books following the adventures of the two fearless elves Podge and Dodge.

A young boy named David, on holiday at his grandparent's in Arbroath, Scotland. Has a dream that he meets up with Podge and Dodge on the beach at Lunan Bay.

And the elves use some of their magic powders to make his plastic submarine so big, that they are all able to get inside.

They then have an adventure beneath the sea, where they meet Nessy the Loch Ness monster.

Story Number Three

Podge and Dodge come across a fox cub,
which has been injured escaping from a fox
hunting party.

They look after the cub for some months,
during which time they become very good friends.

Until the time one night when they meet up with
the cub's mother and they have to part.